NOAH'S MITTENS

The Story of Felt

by Lise Lunge-Larsen
Illustrated by Matthew Trueman

HOUGHTON MIFFLIN COMPANY

Boston 2006

References

When my friend Marlys Johnson told me that Noah discovered felt on board the ark, I immediately set about imagining just how this could have happened. In creating this story, I was helped by the following references:

Ginzberg, Louis. *Legends of the Bible*. Philadelphia: Jewish Publication Society of America, 1992.

Laufer, Berthold. "The Early History of Felt," *American Anthropologist*, new series, vol. 32, no. 1.

Leach, Maria, ed. *Funk and Wagnalls Standard Dictionary of Folklore, Mythology and Legend*. New York: Funk and Wagnalls, 1950.

www.houghtonmifflinbooks.com

The text of this book is set in ITC Galliard.
The illlustrations are mixed media using pencil, gouache, acrylics, and collage, with an overglaze of oil paint.
Book design and art direction by Carol Goldenberg

Library of Congress Cataloging-in-Publication Data
Lunge-Larsen, Lise.
Noah's mittens: the story of felt / by Lise Lunge-Larsen ; illustrated by Matthew Trueman.
p. cm.
Summary: During the long, arduous voyage of the ark, Noah discovers that the sheep's wool has become matted into a strange material, for which he finds a practical use once the ark has come to rest atop a mountain.
Includes bibliographical references (p.).
ISBN 0-618-32950-1 (hardcover)
[1. Felt—Fiction. 2. Noah (Biblical figure)—Fiction. 3. Noah's ark—Fiction. 4. Animals—Fiction.] I. Trueman, Matthew ill. II. Title.
PZ7.L979117No 2005
[Fic]—dc22
2004020552

ISBN-13: 978-0-618-32950-2

Printed in Malaysia
TWP 10 9 8 7 6 5 4 3 2 1

To Marlys, who inspired this story
—L.L.L.

For my parents
—M.T.

WHEN NOAH WAS BORN the angels burst into song and the sun rose an hour early, for this baby would grow up to do wonderful things.

And Noah did. He invented the plow and the scythe and all the tools for cultivating the soil so that people didn't have to work the land with their bare hands. And if he couldn't figure something out, Noah wasn't afraid to ask questions.

So when God told him to build an ark, Noah immediately asked, "How am I to gather enough wood for an ark? There isn't a tree in sight for hundreds of miles."

And later, "Actually, Lord, I don't know *how* to build an ark. I've never seen one before. I'll need help."

And then, "Lord, how can I gather two of every kind of animal in the whole world? The world is a very big place, and besides, I don't think the animals will listen to me."

"I have a plan," said God.

With God's help, Noah was able to build the ark. When it was finished and the animals safely on board, God bolted the door shut. At that moment, lightning split open the sky, thunder cracked, and the rain began to pelt down.

It rained and it rained and it rained. Outside the ark, everything disappeared under water. Inside the ark? Well, it really was a zoo. It started out all right, with the beasts on the first floor, the birds on the second, and Noah with his family on the third. Each person had a task to do: cleaning, feeding, and watering the animals, calming them down, and settling disputes. It was busy, but they managed.

But then the winds began to howl. Huge waves rose and fell, tossing the ark around. People and animals tumbled about like peas in a pot of boiling water. To make matters worse, it soon became very hot. Noah had sealed the boat with pitch to prevent rain and seawater from leaking in, which was a terrific idea, except that it meant no moisture or heat could escape either. The ark grew to be as hot as a steam bath.

The lions and tigers got seasick, which was a good thing, as they lost their appetite. The oxen lowed in misery, because having four stomachs makes being seasick especially awful. The elephants couldn't stop sneezing. The birds flapped their wings and screeched constantly. The mice gnawed incessantly on the rafters. And the snakes and the reptiles curled up in the corners and refused to wake up.

Of all the animals, the sheep suffered the most. Their wooly coats, so useful in the cool mountains, now made them utterly miserable. At last they could bear the heat no longer.

"We are so hot. Please help us, Noah," they bleated plaintively. When Noah arrived from the third floor, he was flabbergasted.

"My goodness! What happened to you?" he exclaimed, for the sheep looked different. Their soft wool had disappeared! Now each sheep was covered by a dense, thick cloth, which fitted so tightly around them that the poor animals looked half strangled.

Alarmed and curious, Noah touched the strange wool. It was firm, almost stiff, and not fluffy at all. He couldn't run his fingers through it, just on top of it. How had this happened?

All at once the ark lurched and Noah tumbled down, right in between the sheep. When he got to his feet again, he understood what had happened: The constant rocking of the boat caused the sheep to rub against each other. Somehow the rubbing and the hot, moist air made the wool fibers lock together and shrink, changing the soft fleece into a thick cloth.

And a very hot cloth, too. Noah had to think quickly of a way to cool the sheep, or they might die from heat stroke. But what could he do?

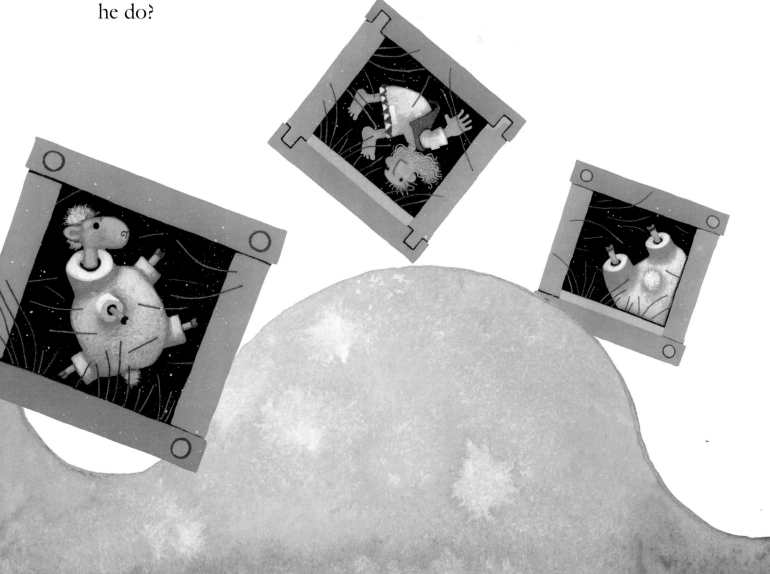

Suddenly, an idea popped into his head. He fished out his shears, gathered a sheep in his lap, and began to cut. The matted fleece came off as easily as the peel comes off a ripe orange. Holding the strange material, Noah marveled at the magical way the fluffy wool had transformed into thick, firm cloth.

He was pondering what he could do with it when a loud trumpeting and stomping erupted at the other end of the ark. Noah stuffed the wool into a corner, patted the sheep's tender skin gently, and hurried off. He forgot all about the wool, for every minute was taken up with caring for the creatures aboard the ark.

When at last the storm stopped and the waters receded, the ark came to rest at the top of Mount Ararat. You can imagine how excited they all were at the prospect of firm ground under their feet and fresh air to breathe. Eagerly, Noah flung open the door. As soon as he did, an icy blast hit him in the face. He reeled backward with surprise. It was freezing cold on the mountain, and the ground was covered with a mysterious white substance. Alarmed, Noah stepped onto the ground and touched it.

"What is this, Lord?" he asked, dismayed. "What are we to do with it?"

"This is snow," said God, pleased. "I just made it! It is really good for playing in. You should play more," He added.

"But it's so cold. We can't live in this, and we certainly can't play in it."

"I think you can. I think you already have an idea how," said God. "But don't worry. It's warm farther down, just like before."

Noah looked, and sure enough, in the valley below it was all green. Relieved, he called the animals: "Zebras, yaks, xerus, wombats, vultures, voles!"

He had hardly made it to the unicorns before he was shivering uncontrollably. His cheeks turned bright red, his hair froze like a halo around his head, and his toes and fingers went numb. Noah stomped his feet and flung his arms around, but nothing warmed him up.

"T-t-turkeys, t-t-tortoises, t-t-tigers!" he called through chattering teeth. "S-s-serpents, sh-sh-sheep!"

"Sh-sh-sheep, come out!" he called again, and out danced two

frisky, snow white creatures. Noah could hardly believe what
he saw. Hadn't he shaved the sheep? Now beautiful new wool
covered their bodies, and the sheep obviously relished the cold.

All at once Noah had an idea, just as God said he would.

"Stay where you are," he shouted. As fast as his old legs
would carry him, he ran inside the ark and down into the
sheepfold, where he found the matted wool.

Once more Noah got out his shears and began to cut. He cut one piece to go around his neck, one for his head, some for inside his shoes, and, best of all, some to wrap around his hands. Like magic, warmth spread throughout his body. And when he rubbed his hands together, he made another amazing discovery: as he rubbed, the wool fibers shaped themselves into warm pockets for his hands. Noah had made mittens! *And* he had discovered felt, the very best cloth for keeping warm and dry.

Thanks to Noah's new scarf, hat, socks, and mittens, he stayed toasty warm until the last ant and the last aardvark crawled out of the ark. And when God told Noah and his family to go and people the earth, they could live and play even in the coldest regions — because Noah had discovered felt and warm winter clothing.

Facts About Felt

IN THIS STORY, Noah learned how felting works—and guess what? The oldest pieces of felt ever found were discovered in Turkey, home to Mount Ararat, where the ark landed. These felt remains are about 8,000 years old. So maybe they really did come from the ark!

Felt is the oldest cloth in the world and certainly one of the most useful. In ancient times, many people traveled as a way of life and used felt for just about everything: clothing to keep them warm, tent coverings to keep them snug and dry, rugs and wall hangings to decorate and insulate their tents.

Scholars think that felt-making spread from Turkey and central Asia to other parts of the world, wherever there were sheep. By 2300 B.C. Chinese warriors kept warm and safe by wearing felt clothes and shoes as well as felt shields and helmets. Roman soldiers even made armor from felt.

You probably know that felt hats have always been popular. From the towerlike hats worn by ancient Babylonians, to the Reubens and the tricorn worn by Europeans, to the fez worn by Muslims during the Ottoman Empire, felt hats have never gone out of style.

Check your closets and your house. You may find more felt than you expect: hats, slippers, boot liners, jackets, carpet underlay, chair-leg and table-leg protectors, piano keypads, cloth covering a billiard table, felt boards, and of course, the felt-tipped pen!

Otto Eunge Lausen

To learn more about how to make felt, check out one of these excellent books:

Belgrave, Anne. *How to Make Felt.* Great Britain: Search Press, 1995.

Evers, Inge. *Feltmaking Techniques and Projects.* Asheville, N.C.: Lark Books, 1987.

Sjoberg, Gunilla. *New Directions for an Ancient Craft.* Loveland, Colorado: Interweave Press, 1987.

Vickrey, Anne Einset. *The Art of Feltmaking.* New York: Watson-Guptill Publications, 1997.